Mermaids AND NARWHALS

Have fun completing the activities in this book!

★

Press out and create a board game,
a purse, a magical model set, and much more.

★

You can use your puffy stickers to finish
the press-out pieces or wherever you want.
Once you've removed the stickers, you can use the
cover as a frame to display your favorite pictures.

make
believe
ideas

How to use your press-out pieces:

At the back of the book there are fun press-outs for you to decorate, display, or give away.

1 Pull out the card pages at the back of the book.

Narwhal notes
Press out the postcards, write in them, and give them to a friend.

make a wish

best friends forever

woohoo!

Brilliant bookmarks
Press out the bookmarks and the sweet shapes inside them. Use them to stencil patterns on pages 13, 24, and 28.

3 Complete the press-out pieces using tape, glue, and some help from an adult!

2 Gently push the shapes until they pop out.

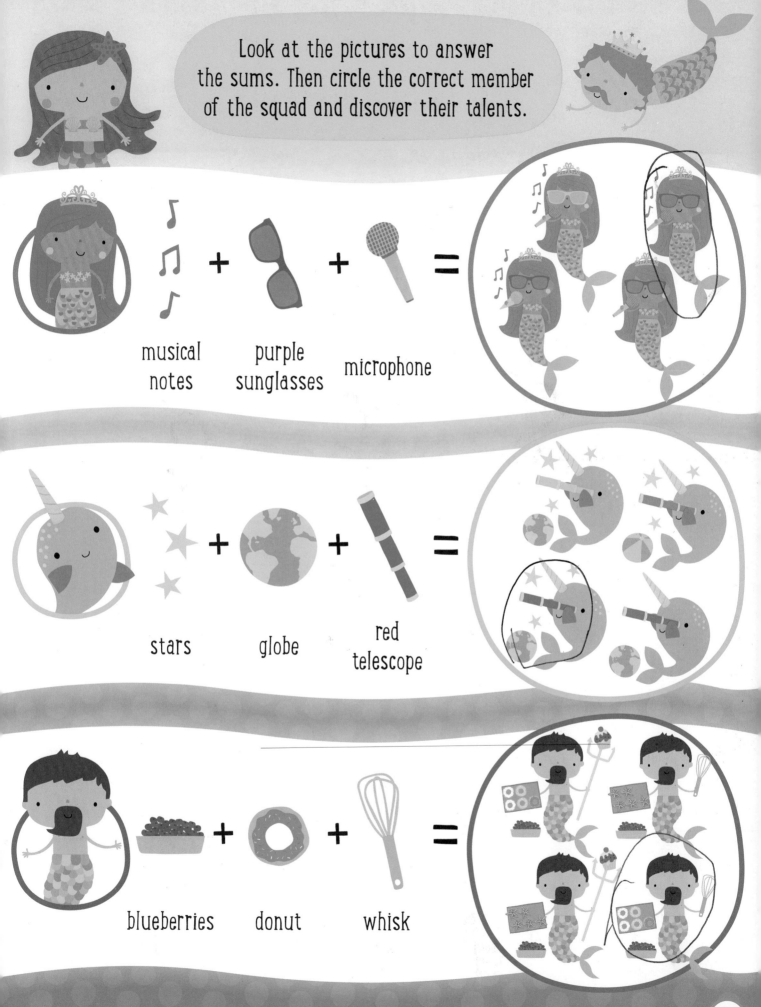

Look at the pictures to answer the sums. Then circle the correct member of the squad and discover their talents.

musical notes + purple sunglasses + microphone =

stars + globe + red telescope =

blueberries + donut + whisk =

5

Kiki's crowd

Kiki is playing hide-and-seek!
Can you find her in the crowd? →

Fishy finds

Lots of tropical fish have come out to play.
Circle the one that doesn't belong in each column.

Swimming lessons

The baby narwhals are learning to swim!
Trace the trails in the water.

Can you find the missing armband?

Color the unicorn rubber ring.

Which narwhal has swum the furthest?

Decorate the
swimming medal
with color.

9

Rainbow Palace

Everyone is welcome at the Rainbow Palace!
Search the scene for the things below.

Check the boxes
as you find them.

1 carriage

1 stingray

2 clown fish

3 crowns

 4 sea anemones

5 lobsters

6 flags

 9 sea stars

Mer-school

The mermaids love to learn new things. Align the letter **A** on the cipher wheel with the **yellow shell**. Then crack the codes to reveal what each mermaid is studying.

b _ _ _ k _ _ _ _

l _ _ w _ r _ _ _ _

i _ a _ _ _ _

Ruby royal

Finn wants a new crown. Press out the stencils from the card pages. Use the shapes to add royal details to the crown, and then color it in!

Underwater safari

The mermaids have gone on a sea safari!
Follow the instructions to finish the page.

Each tropical fish has an identical twin. Find the twin, and then color it to match.

Trace the lines and join the dots to finish the whales.

3.
4
5
2
1

Search the seaweed for five more eels.

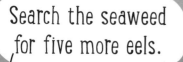

Sports day

It's sports day in the reef! Turn to the card pages to find the instructions. Press out the counters and cards to play.

Start

1

2
You are off to a speedy start!
Move ahead 2.

3

4

20

19

18

17

16
Take a wrong turn.
Go back 2.

21
Get swept along by a current.
Take another turn.

22

23

24

25

7
Get distracted by the cheering crowd. **Miss a turn.**

6

8

9

5

10

11
Find a friend! **Move ahead 1.**

14

13

12

15

Finish

33

32

31
Get tangled in some seaweed. **Go back 1.**

26

27

28
Stop for a snack. **Miss a turn.**

29

30

The first player to reach the finish wins!

Treasure trove

Splash is searching for lost treasure.
Guide him to the chest using the key below.

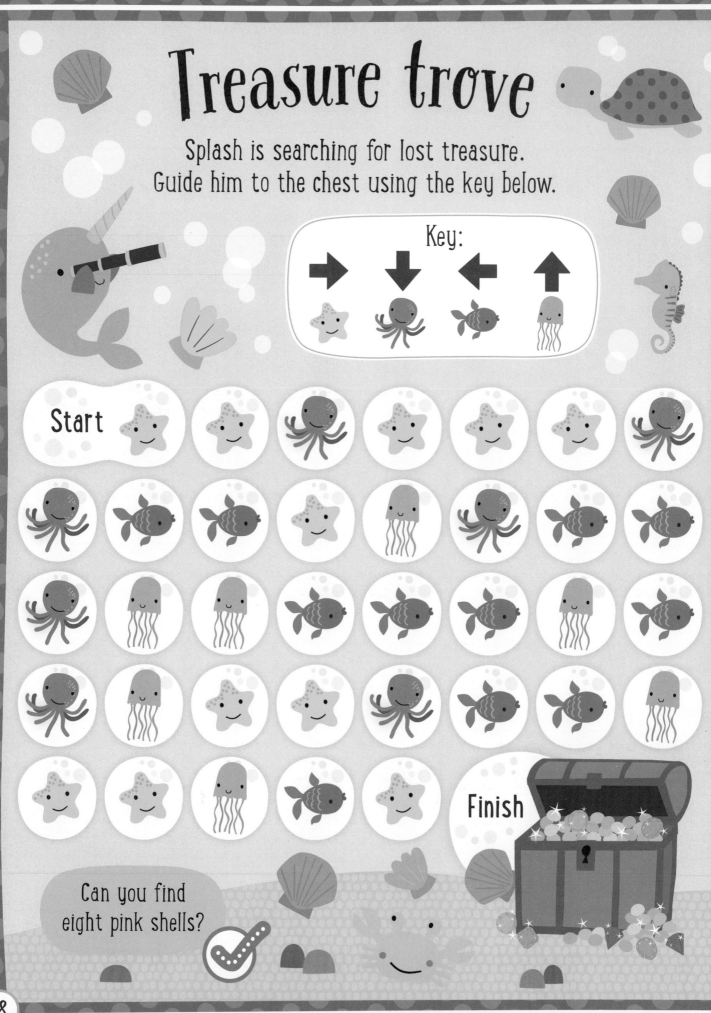

Key:

Start

Finish

Can you find eight pink shells?

Color
the scene.

Join the dots to
reveal the mermaid's
best friend.

19

Tropical traffic

Everyone's on the move at rush hour!

Color everyone swimming . . .

. . . **up**, green.   . . . **down**, yellow.

. . . **left**, blue.   . . . **right**, red.

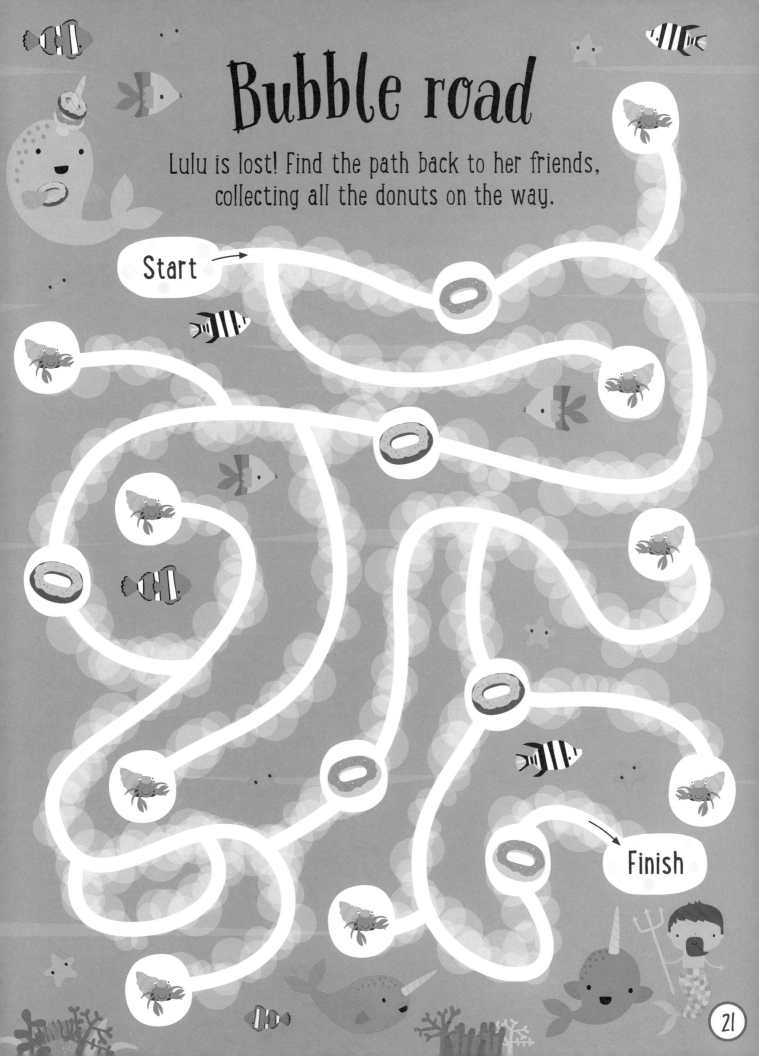

Bubble road

Lulu is lost! Find the path back to her friends,
collecting all the donuts on the way.

Start

Finish

21

Mer-mail

Jonah is busy on his postal rounds. Read the clue, and then circle where you think he will deliver the next parcel.

CLUE

In our home, we love to play with buried treasure every day.

Shell Palace

Balloon Lagoon

Use color to finish the scene.

Aqua Camp

22

Clown Fish
Corner

Treasure
Cove

Press out the cipher wheel from the card pages.
Align the letter **A** with the **pink heart**.
Crack the code to reveal the answer.

_ r _ _ _ _ _ U _

_ _ O _ _ _

23

Pacific park

Glo and Kai are playing with their friends at the park.
Color the picture. Use the key to guide you.

Find and circle five things beginning with S.

Press out the stencils from the card pages, and then stencil patterns on the playhouse.

Crystal cave

Crystal cave is full of sparkling gems. Search the cave for the glittering patterns below. Check the boxes as you find them.

A   B   C   D

Crown count

Alana, Finn, and Coral collect golden crowns.
Count the crowns in each column, and then
write the totals in the spaces below.

Festival fun

The mermaids and narwhals have gone to a music festival! Color the camping scene.

Press out the stencils from the card pages, and then stencil patterns on the tents.

Help Kiki finish her flower chain.
Use color to finish the pattern.

Search the crowd for the
one that doesn't belong.

29

Stargazing

It's a perfect night for looking at the stars.
Join the dots to finish the constellations.

Draw a circle
around the one that
looks like this.

Find three differences between the shooting stars.

Are there more red planets or green planets?

RED .... GREEN ....

31

Piñata pop!

It's Kai's birthday! Color the tasty treats that have come out of the piñata.

Find the sweet that matches this silhouette.

Rock pool party

Coral has organized a surprise party!
Circle the pictures to answer the questions.

Who is singing?

Which narwhal is wearing green armbands?

Who is playing the guitar?

Where is the stingray?

Cakes and bakes

The mermaids and narwhals are baking lots of tasty treats.
Draw the other half of the cake. Then color it in.

Which narwhal has the most donuts?
Write the totals in the spaces.

Decorate the cookies with tasty toppings.

Help Adrian bake a pie! Put the images in order from start to finish. Write the letters in the spaces below.

Start .... Finish

Coral corner

There's something not quite right with this scene!
Circle six animals that don't belong.

Toy tangle

Help the mermaids sort out their toys.

Find Nixie's toy rocket.

Join the dots to finish Pearl's unicorn.

1 2 3 4 5 6 7 8 9 10 11 12 13 14 15 16 17 18 19 20

Trace and color Jonah's teddy bear.

Masked ball

Tonight is the eve of the masked ball.
Which row of dancers matches the silhouette below?

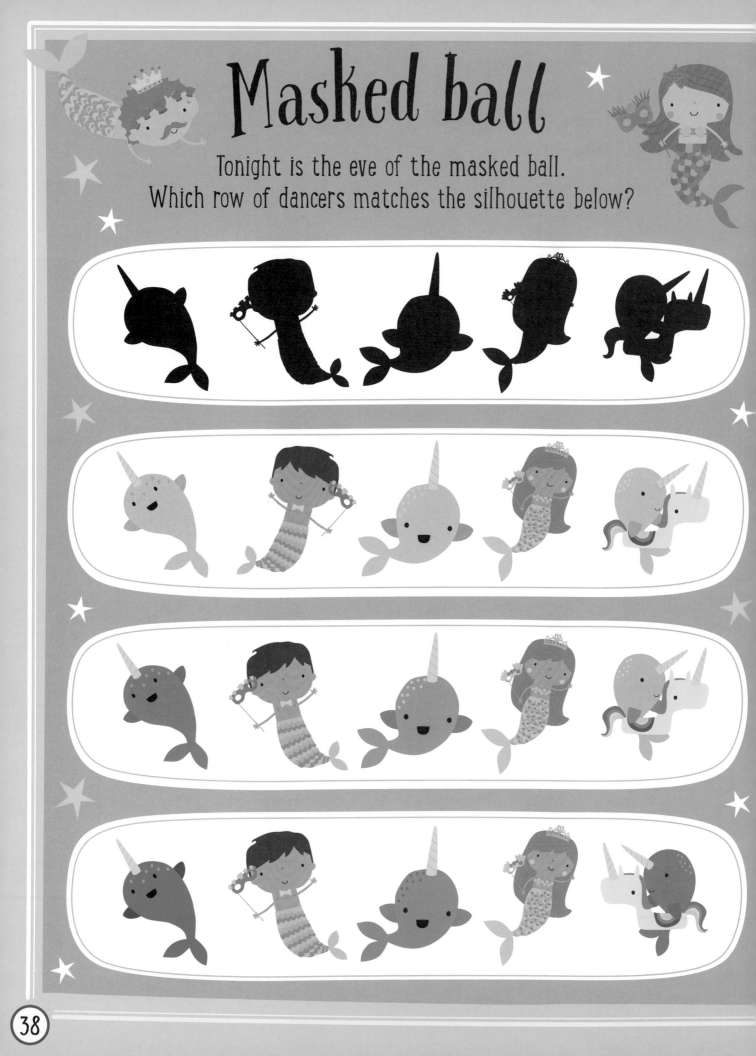

Mermaid mix-up

Follow the lines to see which mermaid has a pet crab.

Doodle beautiful patterns on the mermaids' tails.

Circle the one that doesn't belong on each row.

Can you find ten purple sea stars?

41

Seahorse search

How many seahorses can you find hiding
in the seaweed forest? Write the answer.

42

True or false?

Circle **true** for the things that are in the picture.
Circle **false** for the things that are not in the picture.

There are six orange sea stars. (True) (False)

There are more narwhals than mermaids. (True) (False)

There is only one turtle. (True) (False)

Coach race

The mermaids and narwhals are racing!
Use the key to work out how many points each
character scores. Write the totals at the finish line.

Key:

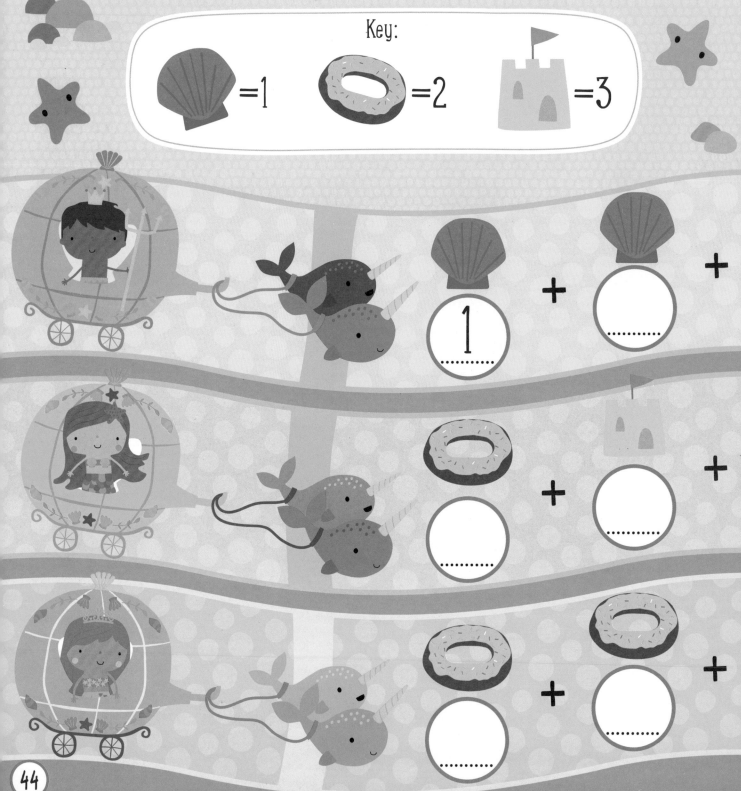

45

Polar pals

Bubbles is playing a game of hide-and-seek with his friends.
Circle the pictures to answer the questions.

Who is building a sandcastle?   Who is asleep?   Who is wearing a bow tie?

Fishy fun

The narwhals have so many friends!
Follow the steps to fill the page with fish. Then color them in!

Summer spots

It's summertime in the reef!

Find and color . . .

a striped
stingray,
blue.

a narwhal
with a donut,
orange.

a smiling
sea star,
red.

a spotted
beach ball,
pink.

a mermaid
wearing a tiara,
purple.

Then, color the other pictures to finish.

51

Pirates, ahoy!

The mermaids are helping the pirates find their way to shore.
Guide the pirate ship across the stormy seas. Avoid the seaweed!

Start →

How many narwhals
can you count?
Write the answer.

....

Color the island.

Finish

Cute crossword

The mermaids have hidden a secret word on this page.
Unscramble the letters to make the words.
Then use the words to finish the crossword.

1 nwda
....

2 aemirmd
....

3 rownc
....

4 aelhw
....

5 shfi
....

6 tsar
....

7 lelhs
....

1 W □ ▨ □

2 □ e □ □ ▨ i □

3 c ▨ □ n

4 ▨ h □ □

5 □ □ S ▨

6 □ □ ▨ r

7 S h □ ▨ □

Which word is hiding
in the yellow squares?

....

Fancy dress

The mermaids and narwhals love dressing up!
Use color to finish the patterns.

Theme park

The mermaids and narwhals have gone to a theme park.
Guide Nixie down the slide. Try to do it without touching the sides!

Start

Finish

56

Design a cool roller coaster for the mermaids to ride.

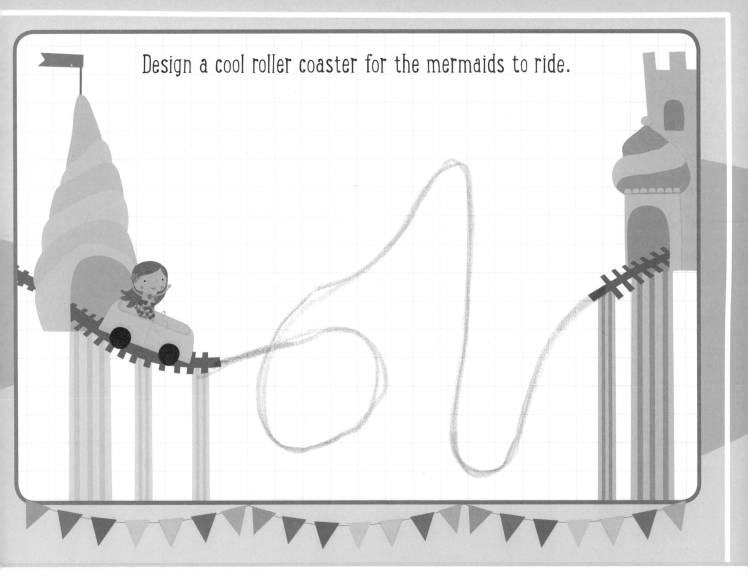

Which square doesn't belong in this picture? Circle the answer.

A

B

C

D

Answer: picture D doesn't belong.

House hunting

Reef is looking for a new house!
Find ten differences between the scenes.

Check the circles as you find them.

FOR SALE

SOLD

FOR SALE

FOR SALE

FOR SALE

Which narwhal?

The narwhals have been getting into mischief!
Draw lines to match the narwhals to the correct shadow.

Sea sweep

It's time to do a count of everyone in Mermaid Kingdom!
What are there more of?

Mermaids
or
mermen?
....
....

Purple narwhals
or
red narwhals?
....
....

Sea stars
or
jellyfish?
....
....

Slumber party

The mermaids and narwhals are having a slumber party!
Doodle designs on the tops to create some sweet pajamas.

Color the
movie snacks.